Chelsea Dizon is an avid lover of children's books and writing. She graduated from the University of Colorado with a degree in journalism but quickly decided she wanted to have an impact in education and received her degree in elementary education. As an elementary school teacher, she has a passion for education and strives to create future leaders. She believes that every child is capable of being a leader and wants to spread that message wherever she goes. She currently resides in Littleton, Colorado, with her husband, two young daughters, and their rambunctious goldendoodle. Chelsea loves to spend time outdoors with her family and loves a good book!

RUBY and ABBY
Visit
THE WHITE HOUSE

Chelsea Dizon

AUSTIN MACAULEY PUBLISHERS™
LONDON • CAMBRIDGE • NEW YORK • SHARJAH

Copyright © Chelsea Dizon (2021)

Ordering Information
Quantity sales: Special discounts are available on quantity purchases by corporations, associations, and others. For details, contact the publisher at the address below.

Publisher's Cataloging-in-Publication data
Dizon, Chelsea
Ruby and Abby Visit the White House

ISBN 9781647506360 (Paperback)
ISBN 9781647506353 (Hardback)
ISBN 9781647506377 (ePub e-book)

Library of Congress Control Number: 2021911810

www.austinmacauley.com/us

First Published (2021)
Austin Macauley Publishers LLC
40 Wall Street, 33rd Floor, Suite 3302
New York, NY 10005
USA

mail-usa@austinmacauley.com
+1 (646) 5125767

I dedicate this book to my daughters, Mehana Ruby and Mahea Abby,

may you always search for adventure!

Pounced – (v.) to jump forward quickly as if you were going to attack someone or something.

Announcement – (n.) when you make a very formal statement.

"Mom, Dad, Abby!" I shouted as I dashed through the front door, threw off my backpack, and pounced on the living room couch. "Moooooom, Daaaaaaaad, Abbbbbbbby!!!" This finally got their attention as they all rushed into the living room to hear my announcement.

"Ruby, dear, what is it?" my mom questioned.

"I had a super, fantastic, terrific day! If I don't tell you about it, I will just burst!" I said with excitement.

Virtual Tour – (n.) is a pretend tour of an existing location, usually found on the computer or internet.

White House – (n.) is the official home of the president of the United States, located in Washington, D.C.

Exquisite – (adj.) very beautiful and delicate.

Oval Office – (n.) The official office of the president of the United States, shaped as an oval.

"Tell us all about it, sweetheart," Mom said to me as she walked to the kitchen table to grab some snacks. "I love hearing about your school day."

"Today, I went on a virtual tour of The White House, it was exquisite!" I shouted again as I tried to relay the excitement of my day.

"You saw a house that's white? And a virtual whatywhatyy? Umm, why is that exquisite, as you said?" my little sister, Abby, seemed confused.

"Well, it's exciting because I have decided that I am going to be the president one day!"

"That's great honey, the president of what, the student council?" Mom had not heard my first statement about The White House. She offered us her snacks in hand, "Let me know how I can help, I am going to start dinner now."

"Abby, we will talk with them later, we have work to do, grab those cookies!" I whispered, to let Abby know that if her and I were going to be the ones in the Oval Office one day, we needed to get to work.

Mahogany – (n.) hard reddish-brown wood from a tropical tree, used for furniture.

"Let me paint a picture for you, Abby," I said, waving my hand about as if The White House was my bedroom.
"There are big mahogany desks, books of every shape and size, and so many rooms. People from all over the world walking around, leaders, and lots of food!" It was hard to paint a picture without showing her the place. "Oh, Abby, I wish I could just show you!"

Leader – (n.) the person who is in charge of a group, organization, or country.

Government – (n.) the governing body or leadership of a nation, state, or community.

Enormous – (adj.) very large in size.

"And if I were the president, Abby, or when I am the president, we will have all the chocolate and skittles we want! Most importantly, I will make big decisions and decide if kids have to go to school and for how long. I will be a brilliant leader and change the world!"
"We are always leaders, right, Ruby," Abby said back.
"Exactly, Abby." As I started to think of all the wonderful things I will do, I began to envision myself, along with Abby, as the most important leaders in the United States government.

"Come Abby, let me tell you more," I said as we laid down on my bed. "When you open the enormous white doors…" As I started to speak, we began to imagine that we were actually there, standing at the doors of The White House.

Grand – (adj.) magnificent in appearance, size, or style.

Destiny – (n.) the events that will probably happen to a particular person in the future.

Approached – (v.) to move near to someone or something in distance or time.

"Are, are, are we at The White House?" Abby looked around with wide eyes. "Now I know what you are
talking about, Ruby, it's so grand."
"Yes, Abby, we are here, living our destiny," I stated quietly. "I could feel that today was going to be the best day ever."
We both approached the big white doors and knocked quietly. To our surprise no one came to the door. I could sense that Abby was thinking this was crazy.

Persevere – (v.) continue in a course of action even in the face of difficulty.

Identify – (v.) establish or indicate who or what (someone or something) is.

"Hmm, Abby, what do we do in times like this?" I questioned her, ensuring she had been taking her leadership training seriously.

"Let's see, Ruby, we plan, we have a problem, we persevere," Abby stated shyly.

"Mostly correct. We identify the problem, we make a plan, and we persevere through," I reminded her. "Let's see, our problem is that we cannot get to where we need to be. Now we need a plan. Hmm…I know, let's see if people are inside." I propped Abby up on my shoulders.

"I, I can't see anyone, Ruby." Abby sighed.

She jumped down off my shoulders and I looked around, "That's okay, we just need a new plan."

"Let's head through the back," I stated. "Our new plan is that we are going to wait for someone to come out the back and see if they will let us go inside," I said proudly.

"We just need to persevere."

Confidence – (n.) to have a strong feeling of trust in someone or something.

We quickly ran around to the back of the building where some workers were heading out the back.
Yes! I thought as I saw the door still open, I had confidence this plan would work.

Awe – (n.) a feeling of respect mixed with fear or wonder.

Vastness – (n.) very great extent or size.

Proposal – (n.) a plan or idea, especially a written one, given to others.

Sure enough, the door was left open and we were inside The White House and in awe of the vastness of the building. People of every age were hustling and bustling and they all seemed to be doing something important.

"Ruby, what do we do now?" Abby asked with concern.

As I began to answer, a mob of people came running up, "Miss. President, what is your thought on the New York deal? Miss. President, did you receive my proposal? Miss. President, are you okay? Miss. President, you look pale."

I began to spin. I grabbed Abby by the hand and we ran into the first door we found.

"Wow, where are we, and who were all those people, what did they mean by Miss. President?" Abby asked as we both looked around the beautiful room. On each wall were beautifully placed pictures of past presidents. We both stood silently in awe for several minutes.

George Washington – (n.) The very first president of the United States.

Abraham Lincoln – (n.) The 16th president of the United States. Known as "honest Abe" and for ending slavery.

Decision – (n.) a conclusion reached after considering several options.

Hesitantly – (adv.) to be tentative, shy or unsure manner.

"Am I the president of the United States? I'm-I'm-I'm way too little." I looked back at Abby.
"No, this is why you are here," Abby said calmly.
"Well, I'm not sure where we are, but I am sure they could help me if they were really here," I thought out loud as I looked at the pictures.
"Okay, now our problem is that I am the president and I have absolutely positively no idea what to do!"
"Well, it sounds like you need a plan then, Miss Ruby," said a solid voice that came from the painting of George Washington.
"What was that!?" Abby and I screamed at the same time.

"You see, before you stand two different paths," the George Washington picture began to talk

"Yes, yes, and you can either take the right path," said the Abraham Lincoln picture.
"Or the wrong one, I already know that," I said back as I stood in amazement.
"No, the left path. You see those two doors, one leads to the Oval Office," he said, "the other door leads out the back."

Racing – (adj.) moving fast.

Proud – (adj.) feeling deep pleasure or satisfaction as a result of one's own achievements, or those of someone you are very close to.

Abby and I both turned to see the two doors that so stood before us. I thought about the hard decision I now had to make."Well, I have never been one to back down," I stated hesitantly, then I gained some more confidence, "and today's not the day, we had a problem, the plan is that I am going to act as president and make the big decisions, and then we will persevere, until dinner time of course." I could feel my courage coming back to me. "Ruby, you are brilliant, we will most definitely stick to the plan, and we will always persevere."
Abby smiled back.

"Maybe you guys can help us?" I looked at the paintings.
"You have all you need inside you," said one president.
"Be strong, courageous, and do what's right,"
added another.

"Be confident, and stick with what you know as a leader," said George Washington.
"Yes, you are all right, if I identify the real problem, make a plan, and persevere, I will be able to make decisions easily," I said with confidence. "Let's go, Abby, I know which door."

"Thank you, presidents," we both yelled as we headed to the right door.
I could feel my heart racing, I knew behind that door was a group of people needing my help.
"Abby, open the door, and follow me in!" I felt proud to be the president.

Agenda – (n.) a list of items to be discussed at a meeting.

Boycotting – (v.) to refuse to cooperate with or participate in (a policy or event).

Business – (n.) a person's regular job, occupation, profession, or trade.

Information – (n.) facts provided or learned about something or someone.

Immediately, the questions started coming in, "What is the first item on your agenda, Miss. President? Shall we discuss and come to a conclusion about the New York deal, or maybe we should start with trade agreement, or the ice cream and dairy problem in the Midwest?"
"Hmmm, did you say ice cream?"
"Yes, Miss. President, remember the dairy farmers are boycotting the ice cream distributers and creating a devastating ripple effect for the creameries and grocery stores, in the end it's also creating a diminishing supply of milk."

"Let's just force the famers to get back into work with the ice cream places, everyone loves ice cream," I said,
hoping I had a good idea.

"Mam, with that new rule they have imposed, unfortunately, dairy farmers would be put out of business, meaning they wouldn't have jobs, meaning they could not afford their houses," the man toward the back of the room spoke out. I could tell I didn't quite have enough information and this would take a lot of thinking, "Hmm, yes, well then let's hold off on that one. Right now, I want to make the world a better place."
"Yes, Ruby, let's work on that!" Abby shouted back.

Politics – (n.) the activities of governments concerning the political relations between countries.

Intern – (n.) a student who works, sometimes without pay, at a job in order to gain work experience.

Chimed – (v.) to be in agreement; harmonize.

"Well, we all want to do that, it's why we are in politics, but we have too many decisions to make to stop to think about making the world a better place," a lady standing at the front stated.
"I know at school my teacher told me to start with one thing at a time. As leaders, Abby and I know that we have to see the problem, make a plan, and persevere," I thought out loud.

"Our problem is that we have too many things to do that get in the way of making the world a better place, and I don't have much time as it is, hmm my plan is…" I thought it over a little, "to do one kind thing for someone else."

"Yes, Ruby, you are right, if we start a day where everyone does one nice thing for someone else, the whole world will get better," Abby said.
I knew it wasn't making the big decisions or figuring out the New York deal, or how to save the farmers, but if I could make one small mark on the world today, my work would be done. "It sounds interesting," an intern stated, "but, I like the idea of doing one kind thing."
Abby chimed in, "Okay, let's persevere and make this happen. It's almost dinner time!"

I looked at Abby and just like that we were back in our room, on our bed looking at the ceiling.

"Girls, dinner will be ready in 30 minutes, there's no time to waste, make sure you are ready by then," I could hear my mom call from the kitchen.

"We didn't get to change the world," Abby started to cry.

"The day is not done yet," I stated back, "and we have 30 minutes. Remember, Abby, we only have to do one nice thing."

Garden – (n.) a small piece of ground used to grow
vegetables, fruit, herbs, or flowers.

Complaining – (adj.) the expression of whining or
annoyance about something.

Just like that, Abby and I looked at each other. "Mom, let's do
something nice for Mom!" we shouted.
I went on, "She works so hard for us, let's do something
nice for her!"
"We need a plan and we need to persevere," I
stated with confidence.
"And a problem?" Abby questioned.
I thought and thought. "That's it," I said. "The garden! Mom is always
complaining about the garden, and those flowers Dad bought haven't
been planted."
"Yes, Ruby, and she adores flowers!" Abby reminded me.

Barreling – (v.) to drive or move in a way that is so fast as to almost be out of control.

"Ruby, slow down!" Abby yelled as she quickly tried to catch up to me as I was barreling down the hall. "It was my plan too!"
"Abby, Abby, Abby, here is the spot! We are going to clean up this garden and make it a better place for Mom and
our family!" I stated.
"Let's get to work," Abby replied.

Melancholic – (adj.) feeling or expressing sadness.

Sprouted – (v.) start to grow; spring up.

As we finished, we looked around and knew that we gave the garden our best effort. "This looks great, Abby, I can't wait for Mom to come out," I said.

"Dinner time girls," Mom shouted as she came outside, tripping over our pup Champ sunbathing on the front porch.

"Mom, are you crying?" I shouted back. "You look melancholic!"

"Why, yes tears are coming, yes, you two are so so so so…kind!" she burst with joy. "Why, what, how did you make something so beautiful, and in our garden?"

We all stood hand in hand and looked at the barely sprouted flowers that we planted in Mom's garden.

"I know you wanted to get these planted, but we haven't given you any time," I said as a looked up at my mother.

Overjoyed – (adj.) extremely happy.

Elated – (v.) make (someone) very happy.

Winked – (v.) close and open one eye quickly, typically to indicate that something is a joke or a secret or as a signal of affection or greeting.

Coyly – (adv.) in a way that shows shyness to give details about something regarded as sensitive.

Effect – (n.) a change which is a result or consequence of an action or other cause.

"I am overjoyed and elated. You have shown your mother great kindness," she stated proudly. "I am going to pay it forward by helping Ms. Sedwig with her plants next door. She loves roses, and has asked me to help her plant every spring. I always run out of time, but now that my garden is done, I can help."
I looked back and winked coyly at Abby, "We all can, Mom. The best part about being a leader is that what you do has an effect on others, and by paying it forward, we are making the world a better place!"
"Now let's eat," Dad yelled to us from the doorstep.

CPSIA information can be obtained
at www.ICGtesting.com
Printed in the USA
BVHW021007020821
613411BV00005B/248